Ebenezer

A sequel of sorts

to "A Christmas Carol"

by Charles Dickens

Warren Bluhm

EBENEZER

Also by Warren Bluhm

Myke Phoenix: The Complete Novelettes
24 flashes
The Imaginary Revolution
The Imaginary Bomb
Non-fiction
It's Going to Be All Right
Echoes of Freedom Past
Full: Rockets, Bells & Poetry
Gladness is Infectious
How to Play A Blue Guitar
Crossroads at Big Creek
A Scream of Consciousness
Refuse to be Afraid

INTRODUCTION

I have always been puzzled when people who seem grumpy at Christmastime are chided with, "Oh, don't be such a Scrooge." After all, while that classic Dickens character began the story as a curmudgeon, by the end of his fateful night, he had transformed into a cheerful soul who kept Christmas in his heart year-round for the rest of his life.

I have endeavored, in this little tale, to reclaim Mr. Scrooge not as he was before that fateful Christmas Eve — a silly old humbug — but as the good and generous man he was as he lived the rest of his days.

The Author

STAVE 1

THE HAPPY STRANGER

Edmund Filliput strode the streets of the Good Old City as if he had some purpose, but truth be told, he had nowhere to go and nothing to do. The more he walked, the more anxious he got.

"No, not anxious," he admitted to himself, but he couldn't find the word to describe exactly the intense feeling tearing at his soul. It was not quite sadness, not even despair, not quite frustration and perhaps not rage, but with parts of all and none. And the longer he could not name the feeling, the longer he walked.

He passed a cheerful mother with her child ringing bells at a little kettle.

"Merry Christmas," cried the sweet little girl as she pumped her hand and the bell jangled and jangled.

"Meh," said Edmund Filliput, but the girl only smiled and jangled the bell all the more.

A young man with a little book was speaking loudly as the crowd passed, and Edmund's eyes narrowed as he saw that it was a storefront church.

"I bring tidings of great joy," the man read from his little book. "Today in Bethlehem a child is born." But Edmund swept past with the rest of the multitude.

Snow suddenly began to fall in great quantities, and the Good Old City was filled with a swirling as if encased in a glass globe.

"Just what I need now," Edmund said bitterly, and he nearly bumped into a man wearing, of all things, a top hat. He had the presence of mind to say "Excuse me" to the man, who had stopped in the middle of the sidewalk to look up at the falling snow.

"Oh, it's no trouble at all, my good sir," said the man in the top hat, and Edmund saw a beatific smile on the man's face. "Isn't this wonderful? Just in time for the merriest of Christmases."

"Meh," said Edmund Filliput, but he stopped long enough to stare at the jolly man, who met his eyes and laughed a great laugh.

"No, sir, I have not taken leave of my senses," said the man. "I just love to see snow on Christmas Eve."

"It's just frozen rain," Edmund muttered. "We'll all catch our death."

At this a great peal of laughter came from the happy stranger, who clapped Edmund on the shoulder.

"You are absolutely correct, sir, it is quite cold," he said. "Come, let's have a cup of tea — or are you a coffee man? There's a shop right here."

Edmund had not noticed they were standing in front of a great window, where they could see tables arranged inside, a counter with stools, and a few people scattered here and there about the room. He had to admit to himself that consuming something warm would be more pleasant than walking in the cold.

"I must be insane, but sure," he told the man.

"Splendid! Good man," the stranger said. "It will be good for what ails you."

"I don't know what makes you think I'm ailing," Edmund said. "I just agree it makes sense to come in from the cold for a spell."

"You have the air of someone who is troubled," said the man with a concerned smile. "If I'm not being too bold, are you in need of —"

"My financial affairs are none of your concern, but I'm quite fine in that regard — more than fine, in fact," Edmund said in a huff.

"My mistake, then. Please forgive my impertinence," the man chuckled. A little bell jingled as he opened the door and held it for Edmund.

They settled on either side of one of the smaller tables, and a smiling middle-aged woman wearing a headband and apron walked up and wiped their table with a clean rag.

"Welcome to the Holly and Ivy House. What can I get you, then, hon?" she said to the newcomers, and the stranger unwrapped a long scarf and placed it around his top hat on the table.

"Merry Christmas, first of all," the jolly man said.

"Well, yes, of course," she replied. "That goes without saying. Thank you and same to you."

"It goes without saying far too often, don't you think? That's why I say it as often as I can. My friend here needs to warm up a bit," the man said. "What do you say, sir? Coffee? Tea? Or, say, hot cocoa would be grand in this weather, wouldn't you think?"

Hot cocoa — with little marshmallows — a feeling of safety and comfort and — Edmund shook his head.

"Just coffee — black," he said, and after a second, a quiet, "thank you."

The waitress left menus and went off, and the stranger smiled at Edmund kindly.

"Not having the merriest of Christmases, are you, son?" he ventured.

"Whoever said Christmas has to be merry, anyway?" Edmund meant to snap out the words, but they came in more of a moan. "People run around like mice in a maze, and the pressure is on to buy things they can't afford for people who don't need anything anyway, and they are obliged to go see people they don't really know or like anymore. What kind of goodness and light is that anyway?"

The happy stranger smiled down at the table and glanced up before responding.

"I know what you mean," he said. "People tell you to smile and say, 'It's Christmas, after all,' as if that explains all the madness. Oh, thank you, dear girl," he said to the waitress as she set mugs of steaming liquid before them.

"Have you decided, or do you need some more time?" she asked, indicating the menus.

"Just the coffee, I think," Edmund said.

"Are you sure?" the stranger and the waitress said in unison, looked at each other, and laughed together.

"Well, I would like some of that beef stew," the man told her and looked at Edmund. "Are you sure you won't have any?"

Edmund had to admit a bowl of hot stew sounded tempting, and off went the waitress.

"So why has the Christmas spirit escaped you today?" the stranger said. "If I may ask. You don't have to say."

At first Edmund just said, "Meh," watching the steam waft up from the mug of coffee. He had been trying to put it into words as he walked the streets, and now he tried to say it out loud.

"It's all just crazy, you know? Edmund said. "Day after day all year, we yell and scream at each other, and we backbite and indulge in all sorts of nastiness, but all of a sudden Christmas comes along and we're supposed to be all sweet and nice and neighborly. It's all hypocritical bull — hickey," he paused to adjust his word in deference to the kindly gentleman. "There's no comfort and joy to be had, and it's certainly not goodness and light."

"And here you are, alone on Christmas Eve," said the happy stranger.

"Alone, yes, and what of it? I like being alone," said Edmund, although his eyes grew wet. "What's wrong with being alone on Christmas Eve? They make such a big deal about it. Maybe I like being alone."

"I'm not here to quarrel," the man said gently. "It's just that you remind me of a sour old man who looked back at me from the mirror for so many years. One Christmas Eve, I began to see things differently. You know, I should introduce you to some old friends of mine."

"Look, it's nice of you to sit down and talk with me and try to cheer me up, but I'm going home after this and I don't need any new friends, not tonight."

"That's perfectly fine, they came to my home to visit that Christmas Eve some years ago; I didn't come to them, certainly not."

Edmund raised his eyebrows in alarm. "I don't need visitors."

The happy stranger laughed. "I didn't think so, either, at the time. Don't worry, young man, no one's going to hurt you. It will be fun!"

"I don't need fun," Edmund insisted. "I just want to go home and sleep."

"And so you shall," the man said as the waitress set aromatic bowls of stew before them. "Ah, that looks delicious."

"It is wonderful; I've tried it," she smiled. "Merry Christmas!"

"Meh," Edmund said as she turned away, but at that she turned back.

"What's this 'Meh'?" she said in a teasing voice. "Not a Merry Christmas for you, then?"

"Oh, not you, too," Edmund moaned. "I'm just not a Christmassy person, I guess."

"Well, you ought to be," the waitress insisted. "The world needs more Christmassy people, like your friend here." The happy stranger beamed as she bounced back to work.

They ate the stew in silence, the stranger still smiling and Edmund still, well, stewing.

When they had eaten every last drop and their spoons were making a musical sound as they scraped the bottom of the bowls, the happy stranger smacked his lips and said, "If that wasn't the best beef stew I've ever had on Christmas Eve, I wish I could remember better."

"If you say so," Edmund grunted, although he had to admit it was good stew.

"And this will be my treat," the man said. "Merry Christmas!"

"Meh," said Edmund, and at this, the man barked a tremendous laugh of glee.

"Oh, I'm sorry, my friend, it's just that you so remind me of my old self," said the man. "I can assure you that your sadness will not last forever."

"I'm not sad," Edmund said perhaps a little too sharply. "I'm just not in what you'd call the Christmas spirit, that's all. I do thank you for buying me coffee and beef stew, it was generous of you. I can leave a tip."

"Now, see, you are already a better man than I was," said the man. "Had some stranger bought me a meal and wished me a Merry Christmas back then, do you know what I would have said? 'Bah! Humbug!' I can hear myself now. And I wouldn't have left a tip! What a sour old man I was, I'm embarrassed to say. That Christmas Eve, I learned to keep Christmas in my heart every day and every night of the year. It's a much more pleasant way to live a life, wouldn't you say?"

"I wouldn't know," Edmund said.

"No, of course you wouldn't," the man said absently, suddenly adding, "Let's meet here for breakfast, on the day after tomorrow."

"What? Why?"

"Well, to talk about what we did for Christmas, of course — and I must tell you, I'm a bit concerned about you, and I want to give you a little something to look forward to, something to live for."

"What?!" and now Edmund was indignant. "I'm not going to go jump off a bridge just because I'm alone on Christmas Eve."

"No, of course not, silly of me to say it that way," he replied, a trifle mortified. "Still, shall we have breakfast the morning after Christmas?"

Edmund considered. "I suppose so. I could buy the meal for you this time."

"Splendid!" said the happy stranger, extending his hand. "Well, it was a pleasure to meet you, Edmund Filliput."

"It was good to meet you, too, sir," Edmund said, and was surprised to mean it sincerely.

"Sleep well, Edmund," the man said. "Or as well as you can."

They parted company, and it was not until later that Edmund realized he had never told the peculiar man his name.

STAVE 2

THE FIRST OF THE SPIRITS

Edmund felt a little less dreary as he walked through the falling snow on the way home. The funny old man had lifted his spirits a little, although he was nowhere near being able to share the man's cheerfulness. This had been too depressing a year, culminating in this lonely walk through the snow on supposedly the most joyful night of the year.

Church bells rang somewhere nearby, and he thought he heard a Christmas carol. Perhaps a service was letting out, and the doors of the church were opened to let out the sound of the choir.

"Angels we have heard on high, sweetly singing o'er the plains ..." It was a children's choir.

"Meh," Edmund said. He'd had enough Christmas for one night. At least his belly was full, although with his luck something in the stew would disagree with him by morning. That would make this holiday just perfect, he thought sarcastically.

He unlocked his front door, walked upstairs, tossed his coat and scarf on the floor, and eased himself into bed.

At first Edmund Filliput lay in the dark unable to sleep. He admitted to himself that, even though he'd denied it, he had indeed entertained the idea of throwing himself off a bridge or some such. How had his life become so miserable? He didn't want to think about it, so of course he could not think of anything else. Finally, though, he wrestled those thoughts out of his mind and slipped into a dreamless sleep.

And then the clock struck one.

That was odd in itself, because Edmund Filliput did not own a clock that chimed. But a clock chiming the hour had awakened him, so he concluded that the chime was in a dream, even though he had not been dreaming, as I said.

Things grew odder, then, as he noticed a light under the door to his bedroom. Edmund never left a light on.

"Hey! Who's there?" he cried, and was alarmed to hear a reply.

"I'm looking for Edmund Filliput," said a voice from the next room. "Is that you?"

"What the —" Edmund leaped out of bed and flung open the door, "Who are you? What are you doing in my home?" he said and then gasped.

The apparition before him looked like a man, but something in its demeanor told Edmund he would be mistaken to think of it as someone of this world. For one thing, no one wears a toga to visit, and the new stranger's shoulder-length hair was white to the point of glowing, even though its face was smooth as a young person's. The newcomer's eyes appeared to be glowing, as well.

"A friend sent me," the apparition said with a kindly smile. "I'm the Ghost of Christmas Past."

"The mad stranger? How did he know where I live? Did you two follow me here? I should call for the police!" Edmund sputtered. "Christmas Past? What's that supposed to mean?"

"I'm here to show you the shadows of your past, that you should learn from them," said the white-haired being.

"I've learned quite as much as I want from the shadows of my past, thank you," Edmund said. "Get out of my house. I told him I don't want any visitors, and I certainly don't need any lessons, especially at one in the morning."

"Oh, you could learn more than you realize, especially at one in the morning," the spirit said. "Come, take my hand."

"What are you doing? Get away from me!" Edmund said, snatching back his hand.

"Now, Edmund, I come in peace," the stranger smiled. "I mean you no harm; quite the opposite. Come here! There, that's better."

The strange being had taken Edmund's left hand in its right, so they faced the same direction, although how it had grabbed his hand was a mystery.

"Now, let's —" and they passed through the second-story window without breaking it, as if the window and the wall surrounding it were not there.

Edmund screamed. He looked at the street below and was startled that they were floating on the air without falling.

"What's going on? What is this?"

"Hang on."

Edmund screamed again as the ground beneath became a blur and suddenly they were flying across the Good Old City, into the countryside, over rivers and through woods.

Just as suddenly they stopped, and they were indoors again. A Fraser fir tree stood in the corner, decorated for Christmas with candles aglow and ornaments and strings of popcorn all about. A rocking chair sat in the corner, and two soft chairs were positioned next to the tree, under which were wrapped presents, and in the chairs were an older lady and a little boy.

Edmund gasped in surprise. "I know this place," he sputtered, and then he looked at the woman more carefully, and his heart filled with a happy ache. "Grandma?"

"Yes, here is your grandmother who took you in after —"

"Grandma! It's you! Oh, my —"

"She can't hear you," said the spirit as Edmund's arms passed through the image before them. "We are but shadows watching what has been. Listen."

"Oh, Eddie," the old woman said, reaching across to stroke the little boy's hair. "It's Christmas, and your mother would want you to be happy."

"If she wanted me to be happy, she'd be here," little Eddie growled a child's growl. "She wouldn't have gone away."

Grandma nodded knowingly. "Sometimes people — go away — because they're sick and they can't fight the sickness anymore," she said. "I know your mother loved you and wanted to be here with you more than anything in the world. But she couldn't, Eddie, she just couldn't." Now they both were crying, one for a lost mother and the other for a lost daughter.

"But see, your mother left you a present," the old woman said, handing him a gaily wrapped soft package. He tore the paper absently and found a quilt inside.

"She made that for you in her last days," his grandmother said. "See the pictures of puppies? You love puppies so much, and she —"

"I hate puppies! I hate my mother, and I hate you!" the little boy shouted, much to Edmund's embarrassment.

"Oh, Eddie," Grandma said, trying to hug the little boy, but he jumped away and ran from the room. The older lady broke down in sobs.

"Good job, kid, you've made everyone miserable," Edmund muttered.

"Well, it was all just hypocritical bull hickey anyway, wasn't it?" the spirit smiled, and Edmund flushed to hear the echo of his own words.

"My grandmother was a saint," Edmund objected. "She took me in when Mother died and tried to raise me as her own. She was trying to make me feel better. I — just wasn't in the mood."

"Meh. That seems to be a theme, doesn't it?" But the spirit said this with a kindly smile, and Edmund knew he didn't mean the words to sting as much as they did.

"If you can show me this, you know my grandmother died, too, when I was only 13," Edmund said bitterly.

"It's funny you should say that, for I was about to take you to another Christmas —"

"No! I don't need to see Grandma die again," Edmund shouted in fear.

"Of course not," the spirit said gently. "No, this is the Christmas after that, in the home of your foster parents."

The swirling of flight swirled again, and another tree appeared in another room, this one filled with laughter and singing.

"Let every heart prepare him room, and heaven and nature sing —"

Edmund's eyes lit up.

"Now this is more like it, you old ghost. It's the Hansons! There's Ma Hanson and Pa and Lily and —" Edmund's voice choked as a gray snout nudged the image of himself as a teenager, and young Edmund threw his arms around the neck of an aged hound.

"Cody," old Edmund said with a big grin and tears in his eyes. "Good old Code-face."

"He rules the world with truth and grace," the family sang, and the man and the spirit listened in silence as they finished the song, Cody sitting patiently and leaning into the young man throughout.

"He's really taken to you, Ed," Ma Hanson said.

"We're pals, I guess," the boy said, and as if to confirm the assessment, the dog licked the side of his face.

"Ew, dog kisses," said Lily, who was a little girl.

"Oh, dog kisses are the best," young Edmund said. "Come here, Cody, give Lily a kiss," and he gave the hound a gentle push toward his foster sister.

"Eww! No, no," she shrieked, but she was giggling.

"I'm so glad you're here to share Christmas with us, Edmund," Pa Hanson said, with assents all around. The young man just smiled.

"Meh," said the Spirit of Christmas Past.

"What are you talking about?" said grown-up Edmund. "The Hansons were good people who gave me a home at the worst time of my life, and they made Christmas special."

"But out in the world there's no comfort and joy to be had, and it's certainly not goodness and light," the spirit said.

"Look right here," Edmund said. "There was comfort and joy in this house."

"Exactly," said the spirit, its eyes twinkling. "Well, come, sir, we have another shadow to visit."

"Already?" Edmund asked, gazing longingly at his foster parents and the little girl.

"Places to go, things to see, we don't have all night."

The mists swirled again, and now it was a cool but not bitter December day in a city park. A cardinal huddled in a barren oak tree, and a squirrel foraged on the ground not far from the park bench where a young couple sat. She was a striking, dark-haired beauty, and he, of course, was Edmund.

"Oh, no, spirit, not this," Edmund whispered.

"It's not you, it's me," the girl was saying.

"Oh, for —" the young man scoffed. "Fine. I can do Christmassy things with you if that's what it will take to make you happy."

"I don't want you to do things you don't want to do, and it's not just at Christmas, Edmund," said the young woman. "Can't you see how we've grown apart? All you think about is getting ahead. You're so intense and focused, and I guess I admire that, but it's so obvious that you'd rather do it alone. I'm just a distraction."

"No, I —" the young man began, but paused as he realized she was right. "I was only trying to make a life for us, Bella."

"And yet somehow I always seem to be left behind," she said. "You only have room in your heart for what you want. You know I'm right." Edmund remained silent. "I need light-heartedness from time to time, and yes, especially at this time of year, without my forcing it on you. It doesn't work that way."

"What do you want me to say? What do you want me to do?"

She stood and said, "The man I fell in love with didn't need to ask, but you're not that man anymore. It's fine, Edmund. I'll be all right. I wish you only the best."

With that she walked away, and the man watched her leave. Edmund on the bench imagined that he heard her sob just as she went out of sight, but

Edmund standing with the spirit could see it was not imagination. Both Edmunds groaned, but past Edmund did not get up from the bench to follow her.

And, just like that, somewhere, a clock chimed twice.

STAVE 3

THE SECOND OF THE SPIRITS

Edmund awakened with a snort and was startled to find himself back in his bedroom, alone. It was dark again and as quiet as a house could be.

"Are you kidding me? That was all a dream?" he muttered to himself. "There must have been something in that beef stew after all."

The visions of Grandma, the Hansons and good old Cody, and the beautiful Bella lingered in his mind like fresh memories, not at all like a dream that fades upon waking. Edmund lay in the darkness with a bittersweet longing for those days gone by.

Dear old Grandma, how sweet and loving she was. And the Hansons — Lily must be a grown woman by now. And dear Bella, he wished he could tell her what was in his heart right that moment, but by now she probably had found someone else to give her the light-hearted Christmas she so well deserved.

It had all seemed so real, though, as if the strange white-haired being was indeed some sort of supernatural messenger from the past. And the spirit had said, "A friend sent me." The cheerfully odd fellow who had stopped him on the street and bought him a bowl of stew — was he behind all this? And to what purpose?

"Meh," Edmund said, but with less certainty than before. Surely the happy stranger had shaken memories loose to be cast across a remarkable dream, one unlike any he had ever dreamed before, but a dream nonetheless.

"Yes, a dream," he said, and chuckled at the creative power of his subconscious to craft such a dream.

The stillness of the household was interrupted by a soft thud, and once again Edmund saw light begin to glow under his bedroom door.

"I am having another dream, about another visitor," Edmund said, but it was more of a question than a statement.

He opened the door to find his living room transformed into a summer garden completely alien to the December cold outside. Green was everywhere, green the color of life, green vines and green branches and green flowers sprouting blooms of white and yellow and blue and crimson. The tables and chairs and counter were filled with holly, mistletoe and ivy, and food was piled on the floor to make up a kind of throne — turkeys, geese, game, pies and plum puddings, cakes and bowls of punch — and resting on the throne was a giant of a man holding a torch shaped like a cornucopia and wearing a deep-green robe bordered with white fur.

"Come on in, my friend!" cried the green-clad apparition, waving his torch in greeting. "Come in, and get to know me!"

Edmund stepped into the room tentatively and warily. The newcomer seemed jovial enough, except that he didn't belong there and that his arrival had entirely disrupted Edmund's living room.

"And you are —?" Edmund asked.

"I am the Ghost of Christmas Present," the second spirit intoned, as if he had spoken thus many times before, but still with enthusiasm. "You have never seen the like of me before!"

"No, I most certainly have not," Edmund said. "I assume that you would like to show me, well, present-day Christmas as opposed to the shadows your colleague showed me."

The spirit laughed a hardy laugh. "Clever little man! It so happens that I do have some scenes to show you, scenes that may disturb you, scenes that may delight you, but scenes that must awaken you before it is too late."

"That almost sounds like a threat," said Edmund, warily, and the spirit laughed again.

"Please, my friend. Take it as a sincere warning. I and my colleagues have only your eternal welfare in our hearts."

At this Edmund laughed, a somewhat cynical laugh if truth be told.

"'Eternal welfare,' my, my," he said. "Sounds serious."

The man in green suddenly laughed loudly, and just as suddenly stopped.

"As serious as the fate of your immortal soul," it said, frowning but with an impish glint in its eyes.

Edmund gulped.

"Well, then, spirit," he said. "Lead on."

The giant man-like spirit raised his cornucopia-torch and took Edmund's hand. Just as the first wraith had, he led Edmund through the second-story window, which was still extremely unnerving but not quite as alarming as the first time.

The Good Old City looked more familiar this time, because this was Christmas Present rather than the past, and so everything was as it had been earlier that day, as opposed to the visit to Christmas Past when buildings that now existed had not yet been built and great trees stood that had since been felled.

"Where are you taking me? Who are we meeting?"

"I think you will know," the spirit said, and they began to descend.

They were in an institution of some kind, somewhat like an apartment building, somewhat like a college dormitory, somewhat like a prison. There were hallways lined with small bedrooms, and as they walked the hallways they saw mothers and children in some of them.

"You are wrong, spirit, I do not know this place," Edmund said.

"You will know soon enough, then," it replied.

The hallway opened into a commons with lines of tables and a large Christmas tree along one wall. The clock said it was still the night before, even though

Edmund remembered hearing the early-morning chimes. A bevy of little children surrounded St. Nicholas, running from their mothers to greet the jolly old elf, who was accompanied by a young woman dressed as Mrs. Claus.

As Edmund stared at the young woman, a light of recognition stirred in his heart.

"Lily!" he gasped. "Can that be Lily?"

Indeed it was, or seemed to be. The gentle face could have been young and eager once upon a time, scrunched up in delighted disgust by a dog's kiss. Yes, the twinkle in those eyes — it was Lily Hanson, all grown up and helping St. Nicholas with the children!

"What is this place?" Edmund asked the spirit. "A women's shelter?"

"Welcome to the St. Edwin Home for Homeless Families," said the Spirit of Christmas Present. "Your foster sister is a volunteer here."

One after another, the children came up to the jolly old elf with wide eyes and high hopes, and he listened very carefully with a wide, patient smile, and Lily as

Mrs. Claus gave each a hug and a gift. One after another, they ran back to mothers who looked tired but happy and oh so very proud of their young ones.

"The mothers look so hopeful," Edmund said with not a little surprise. The spirit nodded.

"This is a way station of sorts," said the Ghost. "They have stumbled for a moment on their journey through life, and the Home offers food and shelter until they are back on their feet and ready to keep going. The Poor and Downtrodden are an ever-changing group, for no one wants to stay down for very long, and here is a place to start getting back up."

"Lily was a sister to me, and now look, she is a nurturing friend to these mothers," said Edmund. "She has always been generous that way."

"Do you see yet?" asked the spirit. "Here is the comfort and joy that you said the world lacks, in the simple act of giving to others who need a kind face and an offer of help."

Edmund Filliput nodded but was silent for a long moment.

"I'm beginning to see what you mean," he said at last.

A woman walked hesitantly up to Lily as the party began to break up, two little girls with bright eyes and Christmas gifts circling her and laughing.

"It's been a long time since my daughters have been able to smile," the woman said. "Thank you so much, I —" but the rest of the words caught in her throat. Lily put her arms around the young mother as she began to sob.

"Go ahead and cry, dear," said Mrs. Claus softly. "You're going to get through this trial."

"I know, thanks to you people," said the mother, still crying.

"Are you all right, Mama?" asked one of the girls.

"Yes, dear, I'm all right now," the woman said, taking the girl by the hand and then pressing her close.

The Ghost took Edmund by the hand, and before he could say anything more, they wooshed back into the sky and over the Good Old City.

"Where are you taking me now?" Edmund asked the spirit, surprised to discover that it took a few moments to clear a lump from his throat so he could speak.

"There is another important young woman in your life, as you no doubt recall," said the Ghost of Christmas Present.

"Oh, please, show me Bella having the Christmas joy she deserves," said Edmund.

"As you wish," the Ghost said.

The mists cleared and they were in a small church, and members of the congregation were holding candles and passing the flame one to another until the entire room was filled with the flickering glow from the tiny lights.

"This will be a sign to you: You will find a baby wrapped in swaddling clothes and lying in a manger," the pastor was reading, and when he was finished, the assembly began to sing: "Silent night, holy night, all is calm, all is bright ..."

"Oh, here she is," said the spirit, and they saw Bella standing near the back of the church. She was smiling, and her eyes were closed, and she was alone.

In that moment Edmund wanted nothing more than to be standing next to Bella, holding a candle and surrounded by the peaceful light of Christmas Eve, singing "Silent Night."

"I'm here, Belle, I want to be here with you so much," he said, reaching to put his arm around her shoulder but, of course, unable to touch her.

"Sleep in heavenly peace," sang the congregation.

They watched as Bella stood in line to say hello to the pastor, and as she walked through a gently fallen snow through the streets of the Good Old City, and as she walked up the sidewalk to 1073 Cherry Lane and unlocked the door. But before she went in, she turned and looked at the falling snow and the good old neighborhood and sighed a contented sigh.

"Oh, Edmund," said Bella, almost to herself. "If only you could have seen this beautiful Christmas Eve the way I do. Merry Christmas, wherever you are, you silly old stick in the mud."

She let out a little sob, and a tear escaped down her cheek, as she turned and went into the house.

Edmund gasped.

"But I do see it, Bella my darling. Oh, my goodness, I believe I do see it," he said. "Bella! Merry Christmas!"

"And I do believe," said the Ghost of Christmas Present, "that our visit is having the desired effect."

And suddenly the scene shifted, and the snow swirled, and Edmund Filliput was alone on a foggy night outside a graveyard next to a country church.

"Spirit? Where have you gone?" Edmund called, but there was no answer.

He jumped as the church bell rang loudly, and ominously, once, twice, and a third time.

And now he saw that he was not alone, as a dark figure appeared at the graveyard entrance and walked slowly toward him, beckoning.

STAVE 4

CHRISTMAS MORNING

The new apparition's appearance was somewhat more alarming than the first two spirits had been, dressed as it was with a hood and black robes like The Grim Reaper. It stood looming over Edmund like the specter it was, giving him the eerie feeling that it had come to capture his soul and transport him away to what comes next.

Edmund Filliput stared up at the dark figure in alarm, but then, a moment later, he burst out laughing.

"Oh, my stars," Edmund said, wiping a tear from his eyes. "I would guess that you, my friend, are the Ghost of Christmas Yet to Come! I'm so sorry to laugh, but you see, I seem to be happy all of a sudden."

The spirit tilted its head, puzzled.

"Oh yes, oh yes, indeed," Edmund giggled. "I imagine you are here to show me my dismal and lonely future, perhaps even my death alone and unloved. Will you take me to my funeral, where nobody comes except the undertaker — Oh! and maybe some colleagues who are only there for the luncheon? No need, no need, my friend, for your own colleagues have shown me all I need to change that future."

The spirit, trying resolutely, pointed a bony hand toward a nearby cemetery, but Edmund only laughed again.

"What a fright waits me in there!" he shouted with delight. "No doubt my gravestone. 'Here lies Edmund Filliput, dreary old humbug who hated Christmas.'" And he pealed another peal of laughter until he was nearly spent. The spirit stood quietly, seemingly defeated.

"Don't worry, spirit, I haven't taken leave of my senses; I've come to them," said Filliput. "Smile, if you can, my grim ghost — it's Christmas, after all."

"Well, goodness gracious me," said the spirit, speaking for the first time, and its voice was deep and pleasant. It pulled back the hood, revealing a thin, bald head that might be a skull's but for the kind and gentle face and the twinkle in its bright eyes that shone almost like suns. "I guess I'm not needed."

"There will always be a need for a vision of the things that may be, things that will be if a person doesn't change course," Edmund said. "You are here to frighten me into making that change, aren't you?"

"That was the general idea," the Ghost of Christmas Yet to Come admitted ruefully. "I have to say, you're a bit brighter than the first fellow I met in these circumstances."

"If he's who I think you mean, I think he did get the message when all was said and done," laughed Edmund Filliput. "Merry Christmas, my friend!"

At that he threw his arms around the apparition and hugged with all his might. The tall bony spirit stiffened in surprise, but then laughed an eerie laugh, relaxed, and hugged the man back.

"Merry Christmas, Mr. Filliput, and welcome back to the human race," the spirit said.

"Please," Filliput said. "Call me Ed."

"I'll take my leave, then, Ed," said the Ghost of Christmas Yet to Come. "I think you have some errands you want to run."

"I certainly do," said Edmund. "Thank you. Tell your friends they did fine work, and —" but he suddenly realized he was standing alone in his bedroom, and it was shortly after dawn.

Everything was the way he left it. There was no sign of any ghosts, there was nothing left of the bounty and the feast, and everything was in the place Edmund Filliput had assigned. If the rooms seemed brighter than they had the day before, it was only a reflection of the light that now shone in Edmund's heart.

"I am giddier than I deserve to be," he cried. "I have to go wish everyone Merry Christmas!"

Not long afterward, Edmund Filliput looked in the window of the St. Edwin Home for Homeless Families. All was as he remembered from the vision the night before — the tall Christmas tree along the wall and the rows of tables with children now cheerily eating their breakfast.

He walked through the front entrance and found a gray-haired woman sitting at a reception desk.

"Merry Christmas!" he shouted before she had a chance to welcome him.

"And Merry Christmas to you, sir," the woman said. "How can I help you? Are you here to visit a client?"

"No, thank you, my dear lady," he said, drawing a note out of his jacket and handing it to her. "I am here just for a moment to drop off a donation."

She glanced at the note and gasped.

"Mr. — Filliput," she said, pausing to read his name off the check. "Are you sure? This is enough to fund our operation for close to a year!"

"I am sure," he said kindly. "And I wish to remain anonymous, please."

"Of course. I —"

"But I would like the donation to be in the memory of Gerald and Louise Hanson," said Filliput.

The woman's eyes widened. "You mean Lily McSwain's parents?"

"Lily McSwain?"

"One of our volunteers," she said. "Her maiden name was Hanson, and I think her parents were Gerald and Louise."

Ed Filliput barked a loud laugh. "Lily is married! How wonderful."

"Yes, she's here this morning," the woman said. "Do you want to see her? Oh, Lily!"

The young woman from the vision had stepped out of the kitchen and was crossing the room toward the tree. She turned and saw the woman with Edmund

Filliput. As she walked toward them, her eyes turned from curiosity to surprise to delight.

"Ed? Eddie Filliput?!" she said, and then squealed, "It is you!" and threw her arms around her foster brother. "Oh, my goodness! What are you doing here? How did you find me?"

He laughed the laugh that seemed to come more easily with every laugh.

"Why, I'm here to wish my sister a Merry Christmas, of course," he said. "And as to how I found you, well, that's a very interesting story."

They spent the next jolly hour talking and laughing about their childhood days, and a young man of Edmund's age — or perhaps a bit younger — walked up and introduced himself as Tom McSwain.

"Why, you two were St. Nicholas and Mrs. Claus last night!" Edmund cried as he shook Tom McSwain's hand.

"Yes, yes we were," said Tom. "How on Earth did you know that?"

"Erm — the fine lady at the reception desk mentioned it after I said I know Lily," Filliput told a white lie.

They spent the hour talking about how Tom and Lily volunteered at the home every Christmas Eve and Christmas Day because of how special the holiday had been to them and how everyone deserved to have a Merry Christmas.

And when the hour was done, Edmund Filliput hugged his sister, and he hugged her husband, and they exchanged contact information and agreed they would meet again, and soon.

"I'd like that very much," he told them.

"We'll be finished here after lunch," Lily said. "Do you want to come see us this afternoon?"

"Not today," he said. "I have something I have to do. But very soon, let's promise!"

And it was agreed.

It was a jolly old day in the Good Old City. The streets were very quiet, as it was Christmas Day, but as Edmund Filliput walked along the sidewalk, every so often he would hear a burst of laughter from one of the homes and the squeal of happy children from another. It was a crisp, cool day, as December days in the Good Old City usually were, but the sun was shining and made the fallen snow bright as could be.

Edmund walked and he walked until he came to Cherry Lane, and he walked and he walked until he reached Number 1073, and there he paused.

Would she be glad to see him? Would she turn him away? What could he say to her? He admitted to himself that he didn't know what would happen, but deep in his heart was a happiness that had not been there the night before, and he knew he had to walk up to her door and find out.

And so Edmund Filliput walked up the sidewalk and knocked on the door to 1073 Cherry Lane, and he waited.

After a few moments the door opened, and Isabella looked at Edmund, her eyes slightly wider and her face as beautiful as it had ever been.

"Merry Christmas, Bella," he said before she had a chance to ask why he had come. The words seemed to strike almost a physical blow, and she shrank back with a sad look in her eyes.

"You don't believe in Christmas," she said softly.

"That was true enough, my love," he admitted. "But I've come to see how foolish I was, and I didn't want to waste another minute of Christmas Day without the woman I love."

"Really?" she said skeptically. "The last time I saw you, you promised to 'do Christmassy things' with me as if it was something of a chore. Has something changed?"

"Everything's changed, Bella," Edmund cried with a huge smile. "I met a man who loves Christmas, and he sent me three spirits to show me how stupid I've been, and I want to spend today and the rest of my life making it up to you. Please, Bella, let's have a Merry Christmas."

She eyed her ex-boyfriend warily.

"Spirits? You mean, like ghosts or something?"

"Exactly like ghosts," he laughed. "They came to me last night, one after another, and showed me visions of Christmases Past, and Christmases Present, and the third one was going to show me my future but I sent him away because I already knew I wanted a different future, a future where you and I have nothing but happy Christmases, every day and for the rest of our lives."

"You're crazy," Bella said.

"No, I'm more sane than I ever was," he said with a smile. "If anything, I was crazy before. Christmas is the one time of the year when the giving spirit replaces the selfish spirit, and we get together with our loved ones to remember all our blessings and all the reasons we have to love and be loved. What was crazy was to let you walk away, Bella. I'm so sorry."

She stared at Ed Filliput for a very long time, then sighed.

"You woke up Christmas morning feeling all alone," Bella said. "And you know what? So did I. Christmas is a lousy time to be alone, but that was the way you wanted it. Go away, Edmund. Tomorrow you'll wake up and be the same cold soul you always have been."

She started to close the door, but he caught it gently and said, "Please, Bella. Tomorrow I'm having breakfast with the man who sent the spirits, at the Holly and Ivy House. Do you know where that is? I would like you to meet him. He'll tell you this is the real me. I'm never going to be that silly old stick in the mud again. I promise."

"Promises are easy," she said. "Let go of the door."

He pulled his hand away and raised both hands in surrender, but still smiling he said, "I can't blame you. I wanted to take you for a walk, maybe go somewhere where they're singing Christmas carols, or just talk about things, tell each other everything we've missed while we were apart. But I also know I hurt you badly, and I'm going to have to regain your trust, so I guess I'm going to take that walk by myself. But please, come to breakfast tomorrow. I swear you'll never regret it. At least think about it."

She stared for a very long time again, and finally said, "I'll think about it," but not with any enthusiasm or conviction.

"Great!" he said as if she had answered with all the enthusiasm and conviction in the world. "The Holly and Ivy House. Merry Christmas, Bella! I love you."

"Right," she said quietly, and closed the door. Just before the door closed completely, he thought he saw her expression collapse into tears, but the door finished closing before he could be sure.

"Bella? Are you all right?" he called, but there was no answer. "See you tomorrow."

Edmund Filliput went for a walk, and he found places where people were singing Christmas carols, and his heart was filled with gladness and joy and, more than anything perhaps, hope — hope that he would be able to introduce the strange happy gentleman to the love of his life.

STAVE 5

BOXING DAY

The little bell jingled as Edmund Filliput opened the door to the Holly and Ivy House, which was bustling with activity as if it were the day after Christmas, because, of course, it was. He saw the same middle-aged waitress with her headband and apron who had served them two days earlier.

"Merry Christmas," he said, and she smiled back in recognition.

"Now, that's better, son," she said. "Had a change of attitude over the holiday, have we?"

"You have no idea," he said. "Is my friend here? I see the spot we had the other day is taken."

"There's a table toward the back," the waitress said. "He and the others said to expect you."

"The others?" Edmund said, hopefully. "Is one a woman?"

"Afraid not, dearie," she replied, and his heart sank a little. "But you never know. The day is still young."

The peculiar old man stood up with a grin as Edmund approached the table. It was a round table, with five chairs. Two other, younger men were sitting on either side of the cheerful man.

"Edmund! How was your Christmas?" he cried, and he laughed with surprise and delight as Edmund Filliput wrapped him in a bear hug. "Oh my! It seems to have gone well."

"Merry Christmas, sir," Edmund said, eyes glistening through a gigantic grin. "You know, I don't know your name."

"Let's rectify that at once," said the man, motioning for his young friend to take a seat. "Ebenezer Scrooge," he said, extending a hand across the table.

"As in Scrooge, Marley & Cratchit, the financial company?"

"The very same," said the happy man. "This is my partner, Tim Cratchit, and my nephew, Fred." Hands were extended and shaken all around. "I'm pleased that you've heard of our firm."

"Why, Scrooge, Marley & Cratchit is well known across the industry," Edmund said. "It's a very reputable company, and I might add very generous."

"I should say so," said Tim Cratchit. "Mr. Scrooge has designated at least a tenth of our profits to charitable organizations for many, many years."

"I'm well aware," Filliput said. "And what about you, Fred? Are you part of the firm, too?"

"Oh, no," laughed the other young man. "I have no talent with numbers. My uncle and I have been having breakfast on Boxing Day for, what has it been, uncle, fifteen or twenty years? Ever since that incredible Christmas when you came to your senses."

"I think I understand," said Edmund. "Was that the night you met your three friends?"

Scrooge laughed his hearty laugh. "It was indeed. From the look on your face and that hug, they found their way to your house the other night."

Cratchit raised his eyebrows. "So! They ARE real," he said. "He has told me the story, of course, but I must say it always seemed a little fantastic, and these ghostly friends never came to me."

"They didn't need to come to you, my boy," Scrooge said, patting Tim on the shoulder. "You already knew all about the meaning of Christmas." He looked across at Edmund. "Tim here has been with me since he came of age, and he took the place of his late father as my partner."

"Tell me, you didn't see an incredibly beautiful woman, looking for me?" Edmund said, which made the three other men laugh some more, until they sensed how serious he was.

"No, lad, I'm afraid not," Scrooge said. "Should we be watching for her?"

"Well, I asked her to come meet you this morning," Filliput said. "She wasn't entirely sure she would."

"It's always a pleasure to meet a beautiful woman," Fred said, "although our wives would not be pleased."

"Mr. Scrooge, I have to ask," said Edmund. "Why did you stop me in the street on Christmas Eve? And how did you know my name?"

The old man grew quieter, though his eyes still twinkled.

"As you now understand, I was visited by the three spirits these seventeen years ago now," said Scrooge. "Oh, I was a mean-spirited, bitter man, only a little older than you are today, but you wouldn't know it because my meanness aged me. It turned my life around, and every day feels like Christmas nowadays. Anyway, I always make a point to walk about the Good Old City on Christmas Eve especially, in case I happen to meet a man who hates Christmas as much as I once did. Sometimes I don't, but this year I certainly did, didn't I?"

"And my name — how did you know my name?"

Scrooge winked. "I sent three ghosts to haunt you, and the only magic that mystifies you is how I knew your name?" They all laughed again, and Edmund conceded that Scrooge had a point. "So tell us what happened after we had our stew the other day."

And so Edmund told the tale, from the arrival of the first spirit — Ebenezer guffawed at his reaction to finding himself flying through the air over the Good Old City — through his long walk around the town on Christmas Day after the awkward visit at Bella's door.

"It seems you are a wiser lad than I was, not needing a glimpse of your future," Ebenezer said. "I never really got to know the third spirit. He didn't say a word, and he scared me half to death. He sounds like a nice fellow after all."

"He did seem relieved not to be needed," Edmund said.

"And your girl," Scrooge said gently. "Why did you ask her to our breakfast?"

"Well, of course, I wanted her to meet you, sir," said Filliput. "I wanted her to see the man who set me on the path to understanding."

"Understanding what?"

"Understanding the meaning of Christmas, of course. I was scowling around town not seeing anything at all. I realize now that Christmas is about giving, about sharing with the people we love, and about being grateful for all we have, whether it's just a little or it's everything we could ever desire," Edmund said, and happy tears started flowing from his eyes. "And it may be too late for me to make it up to the people I hurt, but it's not too late to be a better man from this day forward. You've shown me how to keep Christmas in my heart all the time, and I'm going to try to keep the spirit of giving and Christmas alive all the time for the rest of my life. And I thank you for bumping into me on the street, for buying me coffee and beef stew, and for asking your ghostly friends to visit with me on Christmas Eve."

He paused there, expecting Mr. Scrooge to reply, but he saw that the other three men were no longer looking at him. Their eyes rested above and behind him, and their faces reflected something like gratitude and something like pleasure.

Edmund Filliput turned around to see Bella, her face wet with tears and the biggest smile ever smiled beaming down at him.

He leapt to his feet and wrapped his arms around his beloved, and she whispered, "Oh, Edmund, I —" but she could not complete the sentence. They laughed and they cried together for a very long time.

It probably is not necessary to say that Edmund Filliput was better than his word. For the rest of his life it was said that beyond Ebenezer Scrooge, there was not a man in the Good Old City who kept Christmas in his heart more completely than did Edmund Filliput, and that there likely was no one in the Good Old City who was as loved as Isabella Filliput or their children and grandchildren.

Lily and Tom McSwain and the Filliputs, and Scrooges and the Cratchits, became dearest of friends, and the St. Edwin Home for Homeless Families never had a grander benefactor than Edmund. Every Christmas Eve, Edmund Filliput and his friend Ebenezer roamed the streets of the Good Old City searching for people whose hearts were in need of a little Christmas, and when they found those lost souls, they put them in touch with three very good friends.

It was said most of all that Edmund Filliput understood the power of giving as much as anyone did, and especially at Christmastime. May that truly be said of all of us, and as Tim Cratchit said when he was just a boy, "God bless Us, Every One!"

THE END

Warren Bluhm (1953-) lives on a small parcel of land dubbed Three Willows, not far from the waters of Green Bay, with two sweet golden retrievers named Dejah and Summer. He grew up in New Jersey but became a Wisconsinite the day he came to Ripon College and saw the bright blue sky above the cornfields. He built Three Willows with his beautiful partner and eventual wife, Red, an artist who painted with flowers. *Ebenezer* is the first work of fiction he completed after Red's passing, but her love infused it with life.

For more information, visit warrenbluhm.com.

9 7 9 8 9 8 6 3 3 3 1 6 8